This book is dedicated to Cambodians or
Cambodians at heart,
from newborn to 100 years and older,
who loves magic and the culture.

Copyright © 2023 Chamran Yiv
All rights reserved. No parts may be reproduced or used in any manner without prior written consent from copyright owner.
Soft cover ISBN 979-8-9855933-3-4

# KEVIN and THE TEMPLE CHAMAH

BY: CHAMRAN YIV

**Today is Chol Chnam Thmey. My granny or Yei, as we call her in khmer, took me to visit the temple for the very first time.**

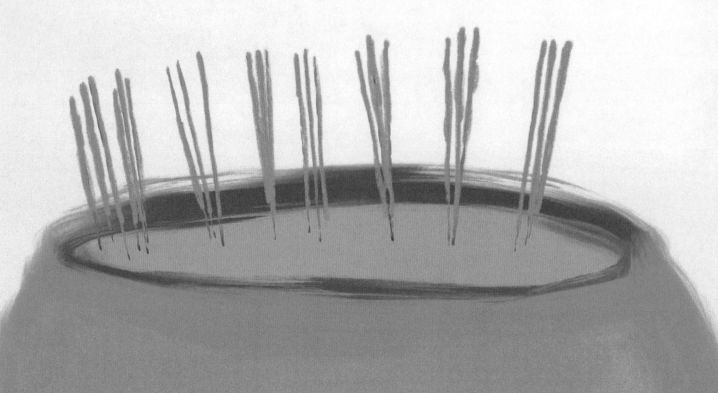

We went inside the temple or Wat, as Yei likes to call it, and lit some incense. Then we sat down on the carpet and Yei showed me how to put my palms together to pray. I had to be quiet and listen to the monks. I really tried my best but I did not understand what they were saying so I kept dozing off.

I was falling asleep for the third time when a chamah, or cat, came and meowed right at me. This made Yei laugh so hard. She even said, "That's a three colored cat Kevin! They are suppose to be very lucky! You might find a treasure today."

**What** Yei said really woke me up. How fun would it be to find a treasure? When the monks took a break from praying and Yei's friends started to chat with her, me and the cat snuck out.

We looked everywhere in the garden and a field next to it and still could not find any treasure. The cat sat down in the middle of the road by the field and said in a soft voice, " Your treasure isn't here Kevin."

"You can talk?!" I asked in shock. The cat nodded and said, "A lot of us do, by the way I'm Pali the Chamah and I think I know exactly where we can get treasure! Let's go visit the sand mounds!"

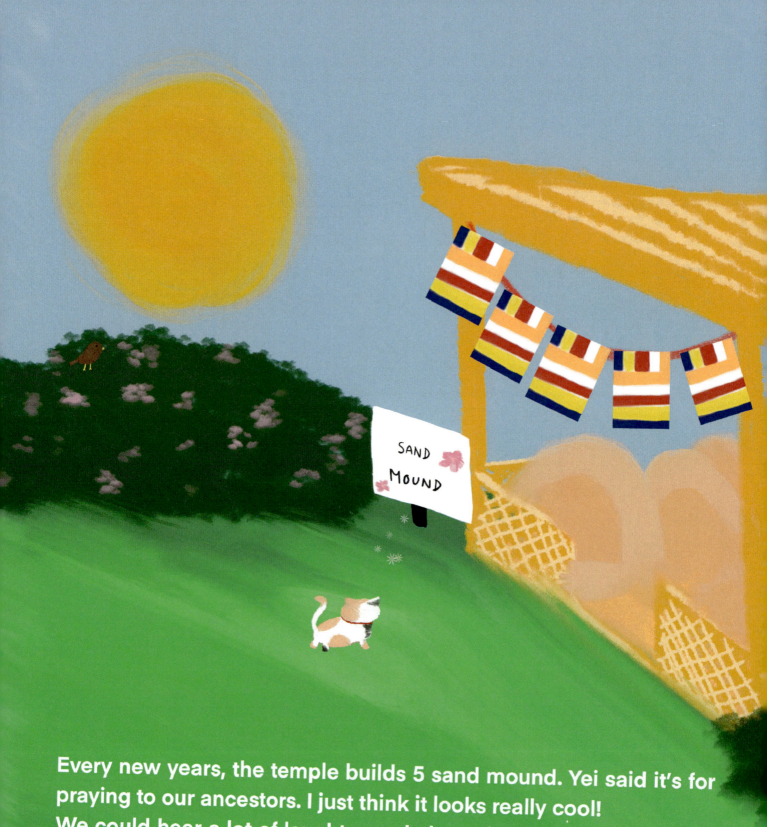

Every new years, the temple builds 5 sand mound. Yei said it's for praying to our ancestors. I just think it looks really cool!
We could hear a lot of laughter and chattering from the sand box. From afar I thought it would be crowded, but it was actually the sand mounds talking to each other! The one in the middle saw us coming in and demanded a rice cake right away.

"We did not bring you one this time Chai, but next time you see us, we have one for you, I promise." Pali said.

 She then turned to me and whispered , "We better find that rice cake for Chai so we can ask her for a treasure. Let's go to the water fountain and see if my friend Prithi can help us get one."

Off we went to the water fountain at the front of the temple. Pali jumped on the stone wall and knocked on the water like a door, three times.

Suddenly a giant bubble began to rise up. Inside the bubble was a beautiful trei or fish, all shiny in gold orange and red. The fish waved at both Pali and me.

"Heya Prithi, this is my friend Kevin. We were both wondering if you know where we can find a rice cake."

Prithi started to think for a few minutes and then said, "I did see one this morning rolling towards the back of the temple, maybe Akash would know where it went."

Pali did not seemed excited to talk to Akash but then Prithi clapped his fins and said, "I have an idea! The birds leave so much feathers in the pond every time they stop for a drink that I have to clear out of the pond everyday. I have to get rid of it somehow. Maybe you can give it to a certain someone and they would be willing to help you."

Pali meowed happily and Prithi swam back to the bottom of the pond. He came back a few seconds later carrying loads of feathers. Pali took the feathers and then we said goodbye and headed to the forest in the back of the temple.

The forest was huge and full of trees of all shapes and sizes. I followed Pali to the thickest tree and she started to knock on the trunk.

From up above a deep voice said,
" who, who, who goes there?"

All the way up high in the tree branch sat a black titoy, or owl.
"Hello Akash! My friend Kevin and I were wondering if you saw a rice cake rolling around back here this morning? We need to find one."
Akash did not seemed to be listening. Actually he started to snore.

"Oh wow! What should I do with all of these soft feathers? I bet it can make a very cozy nest. A warm one too. Perfect for sleeping all day!" Said Pali sweetly up into the trees.

Akash woke up all of a sudden and even turned to look at us.

"I did find a riceball this morning, thinking it was something tasty, but it's not what I want to eat at all."

He said as he came down to inspect the feathers.

He collected all of the feathers off of Pali's paw and flew off saying "I'll be right back"

In a few seconds he was back with a rice cake in his claw. He dropped it into my hand and flew right off again with out a single word. Off we went back to the sand mound.

We were excited to finally be closer to getting our treasure. We made our way back quickly to the sand mounds.

All the sand piles became quiet when we walked in. "Is this what your looking for?" I asked as I put the rice cake on top of the sand mound. They all smiled and then Chai winked. Suddenly something magical happened. The rice cake grew a small cute face, arms and little legs! It slid down with a jolly. "Weeee!"

Everyone laughed and then Chai said, "Someone has been looking for this little guy all day"
From the back of one of the other sand mound walked out a giant Nom Som. It's a type of rice cake but it's longer shape. This one had pinkish red strings to keep the leaves of its dress together.

It yelled "Ahthur!", which means munchkin in khmer when it saw the little rice cake. The little rice cake yelled, "Mama!" excitedly back and ran strait to its mother. They look so happy to be together.

Mama rice cake thanked all of us for helping to find Ahthur. Then she did something really nice afterwards. She tied one of her pinkish red string around my wrist and told me this was a type of master key. It would let me be able to visit them anytime I came to the temple. After that, she gave Pali a small ball of yarn.

I was very happy to find my treasure but I was even happier to know that I have so many friends at the temple now, especially my favorite chamah Pali. I said goodbye and left with Pali to go back to Yei. I was starting to miss her too.

We went back inside the temple and sat down next to Yei. We tried to pray again. I watched Pali sleeping on Yei's lap and that made me feel tired too.

Made in the USA
Middletown, DE
13 April 2023